Stranded!

The tornado of dust and wind swallowed the tower for ten seconds. It hit the long iron vane of the mill against which the boy leaned. Instinctively, to keep from being hurled off the platform, he seized the vane. It revolved twice, making complete circles. The first circle slid him to its end, beyond the platform. On the second circle, both his legs struck the wooden platform just above his ankles.

When the ten seconds were over, and the dust devil had passed on, he was hanging by his hands from the vane thirty feet in the air.

Whichaway

Whichaway

by
Glendon and Kathryn Swarthout

with decorations by Paul Tankersley

BORZOI BOOKS · ALFRED A. KNOPF
NEW YORK

A BORZOI SPRINTER PUBLISHED BY ALFRED A. KNOPF, INC.
Copyright © 1966 by Glendon and Kathryn Swarthout
Cover art and interior illustrations © 1992 by Paul Tankersley

Library of Congress Catalog Card Number: 66-9623
ISBN: 0-679-82022-1
RL: 6.2
First Borzoi Sprinter edition: January 1992

Manufactured in the United States of America
10 9 8 7 6 5 4 3 2 1

"You can go into the ground two ways: you owin' the world or the world owin' you. Don't you go owin'."

— Beans

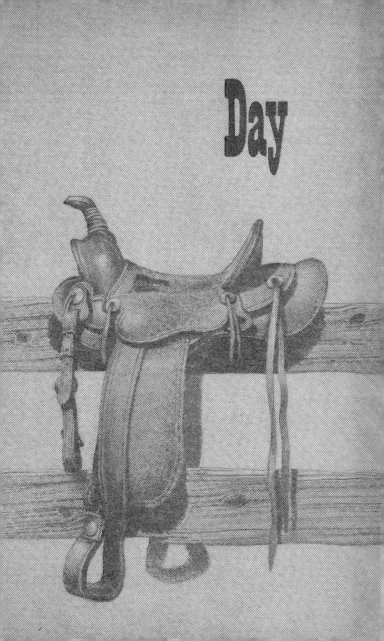

Day

Day

The boy rousted at six o'clock, dressed, yawned outside the bunkhouse to the tap, and poured a basin of ice-cold water over his head as the hands did. That slapped the sleep out of you in a hurry. Then he dripped and snorted over to the cook shack. There were eight hands on the Box O and he bunked and took his meals with them summers.

Nobody said much at chuck. They ate. This particular morning the boy put away three eggs sunny-side-up, a hill of fried potatoes, five sourdough biscuits with sorghum on them, and two cuts of leftover dried-apple pie. To irrigate this breakfast he used a cup of black coffee powerful enough to poison rats.

Beans, the cook, stopped him on the way out. Beans was a sawed-off old gent who'd been a waddie, a cowpuncher, in his youth. Now that he was too rickety for the saddle, he rode his tongue instead and cooked for the ranch and had bad teeth. Once, when a tooth got ornery and he complained too much, the hands bulldogged him and pried open his jaws and gave him a shot of whiskey and took hold of the tooth with a pair of pliers and ripped it out like a nail from a hoof. For his hollers they gave him another shot of whiskey. For revenge he baked the tooth in his next pie.

"Whichaway you goin'?" asked Beans.

"Crittenden's."

"That ain't but five mile. You'll be back t'lunch." With a finger in his mouth, Beans tallied how many teeth he had left and regarded the boy seriously. "Take you a think now an' then."

"What for?"

"So's you'll recollect the world's round an' you're on it an' won't fall off."

Walking to the corral the boy looked over his shoulder up the rise at the ranchhouse. It was a fine house with every modern convenience, hardwood floors and water piped in and carbide gas lamps and bathtubs. But it was a Western house, too. There were racks of guns on the walls and bear and lion skins and Navajo rugs on the floors. Outside, great cottonwood trees graced it. In the winter their leaves were gold, but on this June morning they rejoiced in green.

4

Except for a woman who cleaned and washed and did for him, his father lived alone in the house. Sometimes the boy wished he lived there and sometimes he was glad he didn't.

By the corral and barns and gear shed the hands were already about their business, some saddling up to go mend fences or dig post holes, some to yahoo strays out of the brush or doctor sick stock, two to work on a tore-down truck motor that they were cussed if they could put back together again. They were good men but they weren't real cowboys. Nowadays all they could be was ranch hands. There was a difference.

In the gear shed the boy helped himself to cartridges from an open box, made sure the grease bucket was tied on his saddle and his rifle was in its boot, hoisted the whole heavy rig to his shoulder and staggered it down to the corral. Dub, his horse, was scratching himself on a post, but when he saw who was coming he nickered and jigged at once to the gate. The boy opened it, heaved blanket and saddle onto him, tightened the cinch under his belly till Dub gave a grunt, flopped the stirrups down and climbed aboard.

Once up, he tied a red cotton handkerchief around his neck with the knot on one side. Then he and the horse rode out together looking, they both thought, mighty sporty. No one waved so-long or paid them any mind.

The boy was fifteen. Lately Beans and the hands had taken to calling him "Whichaway," or "Which" for short, but that was not his name.

The Box O was sixty-three miles long and thirty-one miles wide at its widest point, making up twenty-one hundred square miles of range and deserts and mountains. The nearest town was Prescott, which was forty-four miles from the main house. On this spread they ran about fourteen hundred head of cattle. In the good old days they could have carried twice that, for the grass then was belly-high and the water ample. But now, in the year 19 and 23, grazing and erosion had sparsed out the grass and drought had done for the water. The Box O was down to a couple of springs and a couple of creeks which gave up in summer. Water was life in Arizona, though, and what the ranch depended on for its life was thirty-one windmills.

The boy rode toward Crittenden's. This was just a dry wash near two windmills. A family had been caught there with a wagon wheel off—a man and wife and four kids. Indians slaughtered them, kids and all. Their name was Crittenden. That was only forty years ago. History is what you read about. But there was so much of it in these parts, and it was so recent, that sometimes as the boy rode about his solitary chore it seemed to him that he could hear the crash of gun-fire, smell the powder and the ponies and the blood, and taste the bitter medicine of fear. He could feel his heart coil, excited, and like a rattler strike his ribs.

"Why?" he would demand out loud. "Why does it have to be over?"

If you had followed him around a day or two you'd have judged he talked to himself a great deal. He did. And he had reasons. For one thing, he was bone lonesome. He had no brothers or sisters. His father was a silent man, as were the hands. Arizona was a land of people who spoke only when spoken to. Chinning or using too much tongue oil was frowned on. Nor did the cattle have much to say, or the horses, or the wild beasts, or if they did they kept it to themselves.

So this boy did appear to talk to himself a lot, but it was really just one of him conversing with the other. The fact was, in the last year he'd become two people inside one hide, and stretch that hide all he could, it was still too small. Therefore the two of him had much to discuss.

He also talked to his horse. Dub said in his opinion it was a whistler of a day, just a whoop-de-doo day, and why didn't they run a little? He said this by doing a dance, allemande left and sashay right. The boy knew

7

what it meant because they were very close.

Dub was a gray gelding with black patches on his legs and a black tail and one black eye, not very handsome but big. He was twelve years old, a bit middle-aged for critter work, which was why he'd been cut out of the range bunch two years ago and turned over to the boy. He tired in the afternoons, like most middle-aged people, but in the mornings he was full of vinegar.

"Want to kick up your heels, huh?"

Dub poked his ears forward.

"Say, Dub, tell you what. Let's go to Crazy Men Mesa!"

Dub laid his ears back.

The boy twitched him in another direction and pulled down his hat and got a good hold with his knees. He leaned over the saddle horn and at the instant he whumped Dub in the sides with the stirrups he shouted "Hoo!"

They lit out like a cat afire.

They ran maybe a mile. The boy hung on for Aunt Hannah with his eyes watering and scared stiff and let Dub do the driving. For the big gray, the full gallop was fun now and then, and good exercise, and made him feel young again. Probably he pretended Indians were after them and he was a hero horse. But when the boy's thighs ached with hanging on to that half-ton of horsemeat he put on the brakes, snubbing slow and easy. They stopped.

His first thought was, why in thunder did I get a notion to go to Crazy Men Mesa? His second was, because that's the way I am lately and that's why I'm called what I am.

It was true. Lately he'd been bitten by the peculiar bug. He forgot things. He couldn't seem to concentrate. He was given to riding off into the blue—no one knew where, even he himself till he got there. Take now, for instance. Instead of a half-day's ride over to Crittenden's and back by noontime, he was headed fifteen miles in the opposite direction, an all-day expedition.

Dub slobbered comfortably as he rested.

Then it occurred to the boy that he had no food. Well, he'd shoot lunch. When the settlers came out to Arizona Territory in the good old days, nobody packed lunches of pinto-bean sandwiches and jugs of tea for them.

He laid a leg alongside Dub and listened with it to the big heart working. Then he heard his own as something else occurred to him. No one knew where he was going, no one. Beans usually kept track of his route, but he'd said Crittenden's. What if anything happened?

He grinned. Like what? Like being ambushed by

Apaches? Like being held up by desperados? What an ignoramus he was.

But it wasn't entirely his fault. Arizona had been a state for only eleven years and its glorious, wild-and-woolly, shoot-'em-up past was as near as yesterday. The tall tales of the old-timers, and Bean's stories particularly, had put a burr under his imagination. He'd been fed on adventure as much as on beef, and it was no wonder if he was disappointed when he looked around at the way the West was now. The rough was smooth, the untamable had a ring in its nose, every challenge had been met. Life now was sweat and dirt and grease and ho-hum and making meat for dudes back East to eat and that was all. This sad state of affairs was one of the three things he talked to himself most about.

"You might as well say it," he said out loud, "the good old days are gone. The Indians and outlaws and cavalry and rustlers and real cowboys and gold and thrills have turned up their toes. You missed it. You were born forty or fifty years too late. Everything has to change, including times and places and you. That's the picklement. You and the West are just alike. You know what you've been but you don't know what you're going to be."

Dub whuffed.

"Shut up, horse," he said. "You missed it, too. You'll

never rescue anybody or carry a soldier in a charge with bugles blowing. You're an ugly, slobbery, old mill rider's kack, that's all. And unless you want me to sell you for glue, stir your stumps."

Down into and up out of dry washes he rode for an hour through nothing country, over rocks and sand and gravel, between buckhorn cactus and the yucca, greasewood bushes and mesquite. Lizards scurried. Ground squirrels bounced into their holes. The day warmed.

For a second hour Dub picked his way along the lower slopes of mountains. This was mile-high country, and they were going higher. Scrub oak and juniper and salt cedar trees had rooted here. Over the horse and rider a hawk sailed, studying them.

Then for a third hour they zigzagged through the Butter Mountains. These resembled slabs of butter fresh from the churn and shaped by hand. Once, as they climbed, the boy looked back between the shoulders of a pass. He could see for fifty miles. In all that fifty miles there was not one sign of life. There were only sounds. A hoof dislodged a pebble and it tumbled downward, clicking, clicking. The leather of the hand-me-down saddle creaked. Even God, the boy thought, would be lonesome here.

He was what was known as a long drink of water.

He'd grown almost six inches in the last year. Besides being tall and thin he was awkward, because he hadn't yet learned how to handle his new arms and legs. His face had grown longer and leaner and hairs had commenced to sprout on his cheeks and chin which he'd soon have to shave off or pluck out or tie ribbons around. His voice was deep and manly most of the time but now and then, as though a frog in his throat had been tickled, it leaped and croaked.

The rest of him he kept pretty well hidden. Under his range hat he had a bowl of plain brown hair. That was how it was cut, around a bowl with shears, by Pablito, one of the hands. The broad brim of his hat concealed the out-size of his ears. You couldn't tell about his eyes because he had to wear heavy old-fashioned spectacles with rims of steel, and the lenses were always dusty. When he remembered to, which wasn't often, he took them off, breathed "hah" on them, and polished them with his shirttail. Every day during the summer he wore what he wore now: a long-sleeve denim shirt washed to silver, Levis in the same condition, and boots run down at the heel.

Fall, winter and spring, of course, he gussied up. Every September he packed his town duds and was trucked into Prescott, where he roomed and boarded with a family and went to school. It was the only way youngsters from vast ranches like the Box O, Slash Bar

12

K, Jughandle and Flying Z could get their schooling. His mother had taught him till he was ten, having been a teacher herself. After that, from the sixth grade going on the tenth, he'd led a whipsaw life—off to Prescott with people to talk to, sights to see, books to read; then back to the ranch, button your lip, bunk with men and act their age and read catalogues and Western stories as they did. It was whip, be a book boy; saw, be a cowboy.

Except that he wasn't any more a cowboy than the hands were. He rode the mills.

His was a thankless, lamebrain, never-finished task, done in winter by a hand for lack of anything better to do. In the good old days it didn't need doing because there weren't any windmills. He supposed it was important, though.

Beans said it sure as blue blazes was. The cook, who was the most talkative man in Arizona, would say time and time again: "A windmill's like a man. It don't matter how hard the wind blows or which-away, that mill's got t'go on turnin'. The cattle depends on it. An' a man's got t'go on doin' his job, too, no matter what. Folks depends on him."

He gave Dub a breather. Below and before them was Crazy Men Mesa. A plateau about four miles long and two wide, uplifted five thousand feet in the air and benching into a deep canyon on the south, it was sealed off from the world on the east and north by the Butters, and on the west and north by the Dientes. In Spanish *dientes* means teeth, which was what these mountains resembled. The peaks were sharp and savage like the fangs of a mountain lion crouched to spring, to tear the clouds from the sky and devour them. On the mesa the Box O ran a couple of hundred head, for the grass was fairly good. He could see them now, dotting the plain, some near the far windmill which was tucked into a fold of the Dientes, some near the mill directly below.

Crazy Men Mesa was the boy's hatingest place. Besides being the farthest you could go from the ranchhouse and still be on the Box O, there was something sinister about it. It was a place where the winds came to learn how to blow. You could measure the silence with a ruler. Dust devils walked. Humans weren't welcome. Even the critters up here acted queer, according to the hands. They were snuffy.

The boy clucked, and Dub took him down out of the pass to the floor of the mesa and the quarter-mile to the near windmill.

The windmill stood over a deep well. When wind whirled the fan atop the tower, it turned gears which operated a shaft or pump rod extending deep into the earth. Water was sucked up to the surface and into a pipe and through the pipe to run into a big galvanized-iron storage tank. Out of this tank the cattle helped themselves. As long as there was wind, no matter from which direction, since a big vane behind the fan turned it to face the wind, there was water.

The boy dismounted and he and the horse drank together from the tank, enjoying themselves equally. Then he untied the grease bucket from a D-ring on the saddle and holding it by the wire handle went to the tower.

The windmill tower was made of wood, of four six-by-six-inch timbers which slanted up cross-braced to the platform. On one side was a wooden ladder, and this he climbed. The tower was thirty feet high, and at the top was a platform of planks four feet square, through the center of which ran the shaft. When he reached the platform and stood up, he was eye-level with the center of the big fan with its iron blades and the gear box and the long iron vane which stuck out over the edge of the platform like a rudder and had "Fairbanks-Morse" printed on it.

Tilting the bucket he filled the open gear box, thoroughly soaking the cotton wicking over the gears and bearing with cup grease. It was as simple as that. If you filled that box and soaked that wicking with lubricant once a month, which he did on all thirty-one of the Box O mills, they'd run forever. Let the gears dry up, however, and they would burn up, and you had a long costly job of work to do repairing, plus a lot of explaining.

Before climbing down the ladder he looked out over the mesa. Three dust devils marched. In a minute there might be two or six or none. They were high spinning funnels of brown dust, higher than the tower. Like small tornadoes boiling up from the ground rather than down from the clouds, they were driven by winds back and forth, to and fro. You could see them everywhere in the great open spaces of the West, but no one could explain exactly what caused them to appear suddenly and as suddenly vanish. They were indeed like crazy men, starting, stopping, veering, doing what you least expected.

What would happen, he wondered, if one ever hit a tower? They had tremendous force. Beans said he'd heard tell of a cowhand riding along tending to his knitting who got caught in one. His horse was next seen trotting across the Brooklyn Bridge. His saddle dropped on the Kaiser in Germany and started the World War, and he wound up among the Eskimos, wearing fur and lassoing fish.

Up on Dub again, the boy discovered how hungry he was. It was past noon. As they started across the mesa toward the far mill he unbooted his rifle, a single-shot .22-caliber Remington, slipped a cartridge into the chamber, pushed the bolt home and rode at the ready.

He checked Dub, raised the rifle, and got a hefty jack rabbit in his sights. He squeezed. The rifle whanged, dust spurted, and the jack loped away, probably laughing.

How could he have missed at that range? They went on and he reloaded and pulled out his shirttail and breathed "hah" on his specs and polished them. Let him spot another jack and it was a goner.

He spotted one. It was even closer than the first. He stopped Dub. This time he did everything perfectly. The jack sat still and looked at him, interested but not worried. He sighted till the animal was as big as a bull, till he could see him roasting fragrantly over a fire. He breathed in, let out a little, held it, and squeezed the trigger. More dust, and the jack bounded merrily away tra-la, waving good-by with his ears.

The sound of the Remington cracked off the mountains and echoed over the plain as the boy sat there mad enough to bite nails. He'd be a monkey's uncle. He couldn't hit the side of a barn if he was inside the barn with the door closed. He gave Dub a good stiff kick in the ribs and they set out again.

He couldn't shoot worth a noseblow, he'd admit that. But then, he couldn't ride well either, or rope well or do anything a rancher's son was supposed to do. And he'd been given every chance to learn, or rather, had every chance shoved down his craw.

When he was eleven and twelve, his father had allowed him to live in the main house with him summers, meanwhile spending his days with the hands. But since he wasn't making much progress, summer before last his father had moved him bag and baggage down to the bunkhouse. Though nothing was said, the meaning of the move was as plain as the nose on his face. He was a rancher's son, and in the West a rancher's son became a rancher. He followed in his father's footsteps. He learned the business as well as, even better than the hands themselves, for someday he would be their boss. Someday he'd have the land and the brand.

To do anything else was unthinkable. His friends at school in Prescott never gave anything else a second thought. The Curtis boy would one day run the Jughandle, and Moss Lewis the Flying Z. The Box O was his, or would be, all two thousand square miles of it. All he had to do was prove himself worthy. And he had no choice. It wasn't one thing or the other. Out here there was no other.

Well, he'd done his level best. He'd climbed onto wild broncs when he was so scared he had to stuff his neckerchief in his mouth to keep from bawling. He'd practiced roping calves till his hands were raw and Beans had made him soak them in salt water to toughen them. And never a single word of praise or encouragement from his father. But why should there be? Should a man praise a mountain for standing fast? Should he encourage the sun to rise up in the morning?

Another rabbit. This one was small, but a light lunch was better than none. He pulled Dub up. This time he'd make sure. Carefully he eased off and fished in his pocket to find, to his dismay, only one cartridge left. He loaded and, standing beside the horse, steadied the rifle barrel on the saddle. He aimed and squeezed. At the spang, the rabbit leaped and flopped. A hit!

Like a sharpshooter he swaggered to the jack. What he saw sickened him. It was only a baby, about as big as four bites. The bullet had severed its spine so that it wasn't dead yet but lay twitching in the dust, looking up at him from one large brown eye. He had to turn away. But his eyes did not fill and blur until he heard a voice. It was the gentle voice of his mother.

With his finger first on one nostril then the other, he blew his nose, then made himself turn back. That large brown eye was open, but the little jack was dead. He picked it up by its long velvet ears and carried it to Dub and mounted.

What he'd heard his mother say, as she had said

so many times in life, was: "Love every living thing."

Solemn, ashamed of himself, he rode to the windmill and sent Dub to the tank while getting out his jack-knife to skin the rabbit. As he opened the knife it dawned on him. He had no matches! No matches, no fire; no fire, no lunch. Now he really despised himself. He hadn't hunted, he'd murdered. He'd killed sense-lessly, for the sake of killing. Even coyotes killed only for food. He was worse than an animal.

He put the knife away. The least he could do was bury his victim and not leave it out for the vultures to tear to pieces. Since the ground was hard and he had no digging tool, he laid the small thing by a creosote bush and labored a long while collecting stones and heaping them into a cairn over it.

"Horse," he said, going to him and untying the grease bucket, "we sure haven't done a hoot to be proud of this trip. Now let's get the blasted job done and put our tail between our legs and head for home."

He climbed the ladder to the tower. Near the top, a small bird flew past him with a tweet, giving him a start. Peering under the platform, he discovered a nest made of twigs and grass and string built in the angle where a cross-brace met a stud. In it were two tiny whitish eggs, finch's eggs. He'd disturbed the mother finch nesting. Just one more good deed for the day. He finished the climb, filled the gear box and soaked the wicking, set the bucket down and, putting his elbows over the vane, leaned against it and looked out at the Dientes.

Not far away down the range, a mile perhaps, was a draw and through it a snake-track road to the other side of the Dientes, where a back road led north to Prescott. On the far side of that road began the Slash Bar K. But he wasn't thinking about how close he was to roads, to civilization, that is. He was thinking about his mother.

This was why he did not hear the dust devil forming behind him on the mesa. Higher and higher the pillar of dust boiled up, till it was higher than the tower on which he stood. Driven this way and that, gathering strength and velocity, all at once it began to march in a straight line, not like a crazy man but like a gigantic soldier obeying a command, marching faster and faster toward the tower.

The tornado of dust and wind swallowed the tower for ten seconds. It hit the long iron vane of the mill against which the boy leaned. Instinctively, to keep from being hurled off the platform, he seized the vane. It revolved twice, making complete circles. The first circle slid him to its end, beyond the platform. On the second circle, both his legs struck the wooden edge of the platform just above his ankles.

When the ten seconds were over, and the dust devil had passed on, he was hanging by his hands from the vane thirty feet in the air.

Night

Night

He dangled. He could see nothing, he could hear nothing, he could scarcely breathe. His eyes, ears, nose were clogged with dust. He couldn't hold on much longer. He wished to let go, to fall forever into rest and peace.

But something in him willed that he try to reach the platform. He moved his left hand an inch toward the left along the iron flange of the vane, then his right hand, then left and right, left and right. He dared not look down. Inch by inch, coughing with effort, he struggled.

What was the matter with his body, with his legs? From the hips down he had no sensation, except that of weight, which grew heavier. He must see how far he had to go. He bent his head and forced open one scratchy eyelid. He'd have laughed if he could. He'd made it. The platform was only inches below his boots. He let go.

As the boots touched, as he crumpled in a heap on the platform, as he dropped into unconsciousness, a terrible scream was torn out of him:

"A–a–a–a–a–a–a–a–h!"

I fainted, he thought. Only girls and women are allowed to do that. And it's late afternoon; I must have been passed out for hours. I fainted from the pain. But it's gone now. All I have to do is stand up and climb down and slap leather for home.

He sat up. "A–a–a–h!" he cried. It was his legs. He knew then. Driven by wind, the vane had slammed his legs against the edge of the platform. There was no pain now except when he moved because the muscles around fractures always tense up to form a natural splint or support for the bones. Later the muscles would relax, and he would have to live with pain.

Out on Crazy Men Mesa, nothing had changed. Dust devils walked. Cattle grazed. Leaning on one hand, he looked over the edge of the platform. His hat floated on the surface of the tank. Dub sampled some grass.

The boy sat stupidly. He stared at his boots. How could this have happened to him? The chances of a dust devil colliding with a windmill were about one in a year, if that. Why should it have happened today, at the very moment he stood on the tower with his back turned? Was this a punishment? Because he'd murdered a little rabbit? Because he'd changed his mind about Crittenden's and come here? Because he was a whichaway when he was supposed to be a plug-along mill rider?

He stared at his boots until they meant something. "Both of your legs are broken," he said out loud. The sound made him sit up straight. That hurt. The hurt cleared his brain. "You can't climb down," he said, "and you can't go home." He'd have to stay put. "You don't have anything to eat," he said, "or any water." As though the cattle cared, or the dust devils, or the mountains. "Help," he said.

Back at the ranch, Beans would expect him to ride in any time before dark, but when he didn't it would be too late to set out hunting him. That meant he was stuck thirty feet up in the air in the middle of absolutely nowhere and here he was going to stay for a whole awful night. "I am so sorry for you," he said.

Like a child of ten, not a man of fifteen, he began to cry.

The sun slid behind the Dientes. Their shadows approached the tower. Slowly the cattle came in from the mesa to drink. To be sociable, Dub joined them.

Cried dry, the boy let himself down on his side and,

wincing, rolled onto his stomach to speak to the horse. "Dub," he said, "pay attention. I can't get down. I'll have to be up here all night. Don't you go home, you stay right around here. I need you. Are you listening?"

Ears forward, Dub was, but not to him. They both listened. It was a chugging noise. They turned their heads in its direction. Out of the cut through the Dientes a mile away, a vehicle appeared, a small truck. The boy's heart leaped, and he would have jumped up himself if he could have. Rescue! Beans and the hands had somehow figured out where he'd gone and here they were!

But as the truck chugged across the mesa toward him, joy became surprise, then suspicion. The Box O trucks were Overlands, and this was a different make. The Slash Bar trucks were Overlands, too. He fought down the impulse to wave and shout. In the West you were taught to suspect anything out of the ordinary. What was different might also be unhealthy. And there was no reason on earth why any truck should be sneaking onto Box O range by the back way unless it was up to no good.

It stopped about two hundred yards from the tower, near a bunch of eight or ten cattle. It was a Reo. Two men, strangers to him, got out. They walked around the cattle, sizing them up like buyers. Each sidled up to a yearling weighing about 600 pounds. From their belts they pulled revolvers and, with a nod for a signal, put them to the two animals' heads and fired.

He saw it, saw the yearlings topple over, saw the rest scatter and bawl, saw Dub rear and jog away, heard the shots crack and echo, but he couldn't believe it. In the good old days such men had operated high, wide and daring, driving off whole herds and altering brands. This was how it was done now, by men who drove a truck and slaughtered for meat on a small, mean scale. But good old days or now, the deed was the same. He was looking at thieves who'd shoot him as easily as they had those yearlings. He was looking at something he'd never thought he'd see in his life: real honest-to-gosh rustlers.

In the thickening twilight he watched while the men skinned and dressed out the carcasses with big knives and loaded them into the Reo. Taking care to leave no evidence, they bundled up the hides and entrails in canvases and loaded them as well. Surely they'd never guess anyone was on the tower spying. Surely they'd vamoose while the vamoosing was good. Instead, they started the truck and drove to the tower.

He had to see why. He peeked over the platform rim. Near the tank they left the truck to wash their bloodied hands and forearms. He took a chance on one last look at the front of the Reo, at the license plate, then pulled back his head. As though with a hot iron, he burned a picture of the plate into his memory. It was green with white letters, with 1923 in the lower left corner, the slanty ARIZ above that, and to the right the numbers 3–175.

The men underneath him splashed and snorted.

"Oh–oh," one said.

Blown from his head, his hat was floating in the tank! And if that wasn't consarned enough, hoofclops! It could only be that dumb Dub, friendly as always, returning to the tank to introduce himself to the strangers and pass the time of evening.

"Hullo, hoss," said one of the men. "Now ain't that mighty odd. A hat an' a hoss all saddled up an' way out here by theirselves. You s'pose we got us some comp'ny?"

Silence, and the boy lay holding his breath, his ear to the planking. The wood quivered. One of them was climbing the ladder. They'd kill him as sure as green apples. They had to, after what he'd witnessed. If only he had his .22 up here with him, and cartridges. He must put up the best fight he could. The only thing within reach was his grease bucket. If he could wham the man on the head, he could maybe knock him out and off the ladder. His hand gripped the wire handle and slowly, slowly raised the bucket. At the first sight of hat or head over the edge, he'd swing with all his might.

A hat. Now! He swung. But the weight of the bucket was too much for the flimsy wire handle. It pulled free, and the bucket sailed harmlessly over the man's head and thudded on the ground while the boy lay propped on one elbow, the wire still in his hand, gaping foolishly into a face and the muzzle of a revolver.

"Well, ain't you a badger," said the rustler.

"What we caught?" called the man below.

"Caught us a string-bean kid."

"Shoot 'im."

The man on the ladder put away his revolver. "Waste a nickel? An' he ain't fat enough to butcher. Guess I'll just push 'im off." He spoke to the boy. "Say, Four-Eyes, how old are you?"

"Fifteen."

"An' never been kissed. From the Box O?"

"Yes."

"What you doin' out here?"

"Riding the mills. Mister, I need help."

"Do tell."

"I can't get down. A dust devil hit this vane and broke both my legs."

"Ain't that a pity. How long you been up here?"

"Since noon. Could you please help me down some way and put me on my horse? I think I can ride. I ought to get to the doctor."

"The sheriff, you mean."

"No. To get the bones set. If they're not set soon enough, I might be crippled."

"You bet. An' you thrash around too much you'll bust some veins near where they're broke an' wind up with gangrene."

"Gangrene?"

"Sure. Know what they'd do to your legs gangrene was to set in?'"

"What?"

"Chop 'em off."

He grinned and pushed up his hat. The boy had believed that the face of evil must be whiskery and hard, with scars and little glittering eyes. On the contrary, it could be young and clean shaven, almost appealing. This man didn't look evil enough to harm a flea, much less rustle cattle or refuse to help someone who needed it.

"Please, at least give me some water and something to eat."

The young rustler considered.

"You goin' to gab till that beef spoils?" called the man below.

"Shut up. Since noon, huh?" he said to the boy. "Well, they won't come for you tonight. You ever seen us before, me an' my partner?"

"No."

"No, an' you ain't likely to. You're in a fix. I don't see no need to shoot a kid with two busted legs. No grub, no water—you won't be alive to run off your mouth come noon tomorrow. You're done for, Specs. So I'll just leave you set." He grinned again. "So long." He started down the ladder.

"You mean you won't even give me a drink of water?" the boy cried. "That's worse than stealing cattle!"

The man waved. "So long, Runny-Nose."

The rustlers didn't leave right away. From the saddle boot they removed the boy's rifle and, deciding it wasn't worth keeping, smashed the stock to pieces against a rock and tossed the weapon in the tank. They gave his horse a yell and a swat on the rump and sent him on the run toward the ranch. Then, pleased with themselves, they piled into the Reo and chugged away into the dusk, vanishing at length into the cut through the Dientes.

It was several minutes before the boy could accept the fact that two human beings had really left another human being hungry and thirsty and badly hurt up a windmill. But they had. He put his cheek on the planking and closed his eyes against tears. They were gone. Dub was gone. He was alone.

In the last of the light two little birds flew in under

the platform, the mother finch to her nest, the father to sleep on a cross-brace near her. Night followed them. Soon, far out on the mesa, the first coyote barked himself into a long sad howl. Others answered. The howls were borne across the emptiness by a breeze. Above the boy the great fan commenced to whirl, and below him the machinery of the mill to do its work. The pump rod squeaked. From the pipe into the tank, water dribbled.

Turning over on his back and taking off his specs, he faced the boundless night. His throat was dry, his stomach was a fist. Well, he'd have to drink from the half-moon and have the stars for supper. In the breeze the tower, staunch as its timbers were, seemed to sway. It was like being high on the mast of a ship, keeping watch from a crow's-nest over an ocean of black.

He wished for sleep. He was worn to a frazzle. Even though he felt little pain, he couldn't be comfortable. The boards were hard and the platform was only four feet square, so that he couldn't stretch himself out flat. Instead of counting sheep, which no cattleman's son would ever do, he repeated to himself the license number of the rustlers' truck, 3–175, 3–175. When he was rescued, he could tell them that and the men would be tracked down and brought to justice. It was a small thing, memorizing the number, but it would partly make up for his stupidity and the bother he'd have caused. Finally he did sleep.

He dreamed, mostly of his mother. She'd come out from Kansas to the Arizona Territory when she was only eighteen, a young miss determined to see the Wild West for herself. The best way to accomplish that, she learned, was to be a teacher, so she passed the examination and got her certificate and began schoolmarming in the gold-mining camps which were snugged into the mountains around Prescott.

For a nine months' term she earned seventy-five dollars a month, out of which she paid forty dollars for room and board. The camps took the wonderful names of the gold mines themselves: Crown King, Savoy, Aching Back, Lincoln, Ora Lee and Dirty Dog. Young lady teachers in those days led exciting lives, moving frequently to a new camp as a vein of gold petered out or a shaft filled with water, playing the belles at parties and dances, being courted by miners and ranchers and gamblers and cowboys—by everything, in fact, that wore pants. And even if they weren't beautiful they were chased after, for young females were scarce as hen's teeth.

Everyone said that what they'd really come West for was to get a man. In fun, newspapers called them "a mob of mobile maidens meditating matrimony." Laughing, his mother insisted the idea never entered her mind. Why, she'd waited eight years, till she was an old maid of twenty-six, before she said yes to the sobersided owner of the Box O. She loved to laugh. Everything did, she believed. Tell an owl a joke and it would hoot. Tickle a tree and it would bark. And who hadn't heard a horselaugh?

He dreamed again, as he often did, of the day the laughter ceased. She was riding out with his father and him on her pretty mare, Esmeralda. He was ten. They were cantering along together and the mare spooked at a sidewinder or a Gila monster or something, reared and threw her violently.

Her head crashed against a rock. When husband and son bent over her, she was unconscious. A shadow fell between them. It was Esmeralda, come to see what had happened to her mistress, to apologize.

Without a word his father went to his own horse, got his rifle, put it to the mare's ear, and pulled the trigger.

As the boy looked again at his mother, her eyes had opened. The expression in them was like that in the brown eye of the baby rabbit whose life he had taken only this morning, an attempt to understand. Had she seen the execution? She groaned, as though in horror. Was that her protest against such savagery? Was her last thought that all her teaching and her tenderness, her courage and her charity, had failed? Was her last sight on earth that of one she loved destroying another for no reason except revenge?

The boy hoped not, prayed not, but he had never known. By the time they brought her back to the ranch she was dead.

In his sleep he groaned, horrified by the memory, or thought he did, or made some sound, or heard some sound. What was that? He woke with a start. What was that?

It was neither night nor morning, but a gray in-between. Fierce snarls from down below had wakened him. Putting on his specs he sat up to peer over the platform at the ground. Three gaunt coyotes had pawed away the cairn of stones under which he'd buried the rabbit. Now, growling and snapping at one another, they quarreled over the few mouthfuls of flesh and fur.

He couldn't watch. To take his mind off what they were doing he sat motionless and repeated the license number to himself, 3–175, 3–175, and waited for morning.

Gradually the gray blushed into pink. Their breakfast eaten, the three varmints slunk away up a canyon into the Dientes. The breeze stopped, and with it the fan and the pump-rod squeak. For a moment, in the hush of dawn, the boy was almost happy. He'd got through a night up here, a whole night. This new day would surely bring help.

What they'd do, the hands, maybe even his father, would be to start out right now, heading for Crittenden's. Beans would see to that. Not finding him there, they'd ride farther, thinking he must have decided to tend the mills over on the Big Bug, or maybe at Yarnall. But that was east, not west, that was the opposite direction from where he was.

A "No!" was pulled out of him. Yet that was exactly what they'd do, ride in the wrong direction. Only some time later would Beans have a hunch to look for him where he wasn't supposed to be, and they wouldn't see Beans again all day. And if they kept riding east, there were twenty-one possible windmills to check on that side of the Box O. Not until dark would they return to the ranch completely flummoxed —which meant that not until tomorrow morning could they start hunting him in the right place!

"What am I going to do?" he asked out loud. "Whatever am I going to do?"

He looked frantically about him as though seeing the platform for the first time. It reminded him of something. Riddle: what was high and square and you didn't come down from? Answer: a mill tower if your legs were broken or, if they weren't, a scaffold. And a scaffold reminded him of Jim Parker, the famous outlaw, the last man to have a public hanging in Prescott.

In 1898, a short twenty-five years ago but long

38

enough ago for him to have missed it, Jim had held up a mail train near Peach Springs. A posse captured him. Trying to escape from the Prescott jail, he'd shot and killed a deputy, was recaptured and convicted of murder and sentenced to hang. A scaffold was built and the whole town was invited to the party, including Beans. Sheriff Ruffner, known as "The Buryin' Sheriff" since he was also the undertaker, escorted Jim from the jail to the scaffold.

"Hold on, boys," said Jim, cool as a cucumber. "I want to look at this thing. I never seen one before."

He gave it a thorough inspection. When the rope was dropped around his neck and he was asked if he had any last remarks to make, according to Beans the desperado replied: "I don't have much to say. I claim that I am getting something that ain't due me. But I guess that every man up here says the same thing, so that don't cut no figure." He shook hands with everyone and said, "It's all over. Tell the boys I died game and like a man."

A red sun glared over the Butter Mountains. The boy bowed his head. It was time now to tell himself the truth. They were searching for him, yes, but in the wrong direction. Not until night would they realize their mistake. For only a crazy boy, a whichaway, would go to Crazy Men Mesa when he was supposed to go to Crittenden's. Not until morning, another morning, would they ride out again. That would be too late.

"You're done for," the rustler had said. "Come noon tomorrow you won't be alive." He couldn't possibly make it through another day and night. Platform or scaffold, Jim Parker or a boy without legs—six of one, half-dozen of the other.

The world was indeed round, and take as many thinks as he wanted, he was going to fall off today. He'd never thought of it before, he was too young. But that was what it amounted to. Be the guest of honor at a necktie party or hit your head on a rock or get caught in an accident, you just fell off the world.

Since there was no one to listen, no one to care, he spoke softly: "I'm going to die."

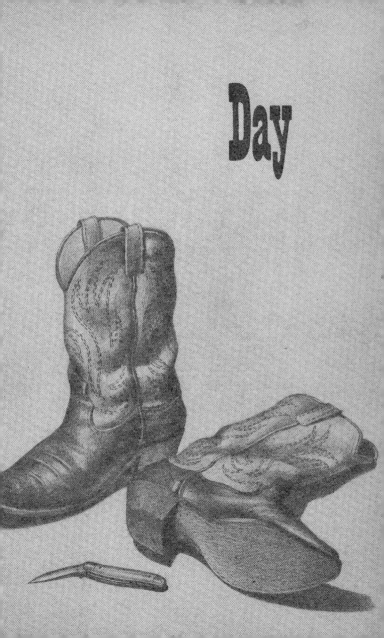

Day

Day

Not with his boots on, though. He couldn't bear to leave them on any longer and he couldn't bear to haul them off. Inside them, during the night, a change had taken place. The muscles near the fractures had tired of the effort to support the bones. His legs seemed to have grown to twice their normal size. Now they pressed against the leather and the pain was constant. If he didn't do something, the boots themselves might burst the way a paper sack popped after you had blown it up and whacked it.

Bending forward, with his jackknife he began to cut at the top, slitting each boot down and spreading the leather. Then he put the knife down and, bending farther, gritting his teeth, took hold of each heel and with a sudden tug yanked off the boots. Still he couldn't be sure what was wrong until he'd slit his

43

socks, removed them, and raised the legs of his Levis. "Oh, oh, oh," he whispered. "Look at me."

These weren't legs or feet. They were fat sausages, horrible to look at, so swollen that the skin was a mottled blue and seemed to glisten from stretching. The broken bones had compressed the veins and shut off the circulation of blood, which caused the swelling. It would get worse, not better. He recalled the rustler's warning that if he thrashed around much, the jagged bones would slice into the veins. They'd bleed and rot the tissues, and he'd have gangrene. And what did they do with rotten legs? They chopped 'em off.

And what difference did it make if you were going to die anyway? He was a prisoner on a four-by-four platform. He was a bird with its wings clipped. He was chained to a windmill tower, like a badger to a dog.

Badger to a dog. In the good old days, badger fights were a popular entertainment in Arizona. Some sporting gents trapped a badger and kept it under a barrel in the cellar of a store and starved it into a fighting mood. Then they brought in an opponent, a fierce bulldog or bull terrier. They collected a crowd except for the sheriff, made bets, prodded the badger from the barrel, jumped onto boxes or clung to the rafters, and let the animals go to it.

Usually they fought to the death. They had to. The

sporting gents had chained them together so that neither could flee. When the event was over and a fine time had by all, bets were paid off and the crowd, spattered with red, laughed and joked to the nearest saloon. If the badger had won, it was put out of its misery for having the nerve to chew up a valuable dog. If the dog won, it was nursed back to health in order to chew up another badger.

You were always sorry you missed seeing a badger fight, said the boy to himself. Are you still sorry? Now do you know how the badger felt? How do you like having less than a fighting chance? Who'll put *you* out of your misery?

Speaking of that, his other self replied, you ought to have a will. Carve it in the planks with your knife. Let's see, what do you have to leave to anybody? Two cut boots, the clothes on your back, a bucket handle, a knife, and a mad stone.

The boots are no good, the clothes are worn out, the handle's useless. Beans gave you the knife and the mad stone—give them back. What can you leave your father to prove to him that even though you made a fool of yourself by getting your legs broken up on a windmill you tried to the very end to do your best? 3–175.

By the middle of the morning the boy began to

suffer. Though he sat without moving, facing east toward the Butters and the pass through which help would come—except that it wasn't coming—his legs, or what had been his legs, began to smart and tingle as though pricked by a pin. Up his legs the pin jabbed, all the way to his hips, was withdrawn, let him recover, then started again at his knees.

He kept his gaze away from the tower, away from his lower body, over the mesa. Cattle grazed. Dust devils formed, took a walk, and spun themselves into nothing. The sun was high in a cloudless sky. It would be a hot day. He would be badly sunburned. Untying his red neckerchief he draped it over his head, but it was too small to cover his face.

His tongue and throat were parched. He'd been almost twenty-four hours without water. Yet the hunger was even worse. It had been more than twenty-four hours since he'd eaten. If he'd had a belly he'd have a belly ache, but all he had was a backbone. In imagination he ate and re-ate the last meal Beans had served him, licking his chops over the eggs and potatoes and sorghum biscuits and dried-apple pie.

"Hee–yah! Hee–yah–yah!"

He jerked. The shouts, loud and triumphant, rolled over him from the rear and spilled out onto the mesa. He squidged himself around. What in thunder?

Down the small canyon in the Butters which had

been at his back came another sound—a tinny, rhythmic clink, clink, clink. He could not see far up the canyon, for it did a hairpin, but he could soon hear a voice raised in song:

> *"Maxine, my queen,*
> *Lead me to gold,*
> *I'll deck you in dia–minds,*
> *Afore we grow old."*

It was like a parade. First the shouts, then the song, and then, picking its way down the canyon, a burro appeared, stiff-legged under a huge pack which tipped and swayed and made the clink, clink as a frypan nudged the blade of an axe. And following the burro came the shouter and singer, the grand marshal of the parade.

He was dressed for the occasion, from the ground up, in miner's boots, baggy pants, the filthy upper half of long-john underwear, and a derby hat which had seasoned from black to green. He was older even than Beans. Who he was and what he did were unmistakable. In the good old days Arizona had swarmed with prospectors like him but they were extinct now, like so many other valuables. Oh, you'd hear now and then of one seen back in the hills, a relic, a ghost who refused to wrap up in a sheet, a very old gent still searching for pay rock, who cheated the calendar with his own cooking and fooled his ancient heart with hope. To smell him was to know he was real.

The little burro came on a delicate run for the tank, her master waddling after.

"Hey!" the boy hollered.

The old gent stopped.

"Up here! Hey!" The boy waved.

The old gent located him, then proceeded to the tank and, shading his eyes with his derby, looked up.

"Straw," he said.

He delighted the boy. Actual rustlers and now someone like this! It was a meeting you'd tell your grandchildren about. Why, instead of being lonely and desolate, Crazy Men Mesa was busier than the Prescott railroad station. "Am I ever glad to see you!" he said.

"What you doin' up there, pickin' apples?"

The boy told him. "So the rustlers just left me high and dry, but I got their license number. And this morning I thought I was a goner till I heard you. I need water most. Do you have a canteen you could throw up before you figure out how to get me down?"

"You say this is the Box O an' your daddy owns it?"

"That's right."

"Hain't there a snake track down yonder, leads to the Prescott pike?"

"That's right. And I'm starving and my legs hurt

like sin."

"This is Maxine." The old gent patted the burro, who was still drinking. His beard was short and greasy. Tangled in it were the remnants of former meals, a bit of bacon here, the crumbs of biscuit there. He fumbled in the beard, found a tidbit, and put it in his mouth.

"My feet," he said. "That's where it tells on you." He seemed to be pondering something. Then, to the boy's disbelief, he took off his boots, pulled from under a rope on the burro's pack a short length of plank, and laid it catty-corner at one end of the tank. Using the burro and the iron edge, he hoisted himself on the plank and with a long, blissful sigh let his feet sink into the water.

"Land of Goshen, that feels dandy." He raised one bare, knobby foot. "Bunions, carbuncles, blisters, boils, slivers, proud flesh an' assorted eruptions—the work of forty years an' ten thousand miles an' the Devil."

"Sir."

"What say?"

"Sir, didn't you hear what I said, about water and my legs and how I can't get down?"

The old gent wiggled his toes and sloshed his feet luxuriously. "Sure did. Let's have us a elementary lesson first, though. I'll ask an' you answer. Now what's my occupation?"

"Why, you're a prospector."

49

"An' what am I doin' out here?"

"Looking for gold."

"Maxine, my turtledove, don't bloat yourself up an' spring a leak. An' when you heard me comin', what was I doin'?"

"Shouting and singing."

"What'd that signify?"

"Sir, I don't know. Maybe you were happy."

"An' if a prospector's happy?"

"He's struck it."

"Hop to the head of the class."

The boy shook his head. It was so ridiculous it made him angry. "That's impossible!" he flared. "People have gone over these mountains with a fine-tooth comb and there hasn't been a real strike in Arizona in fifty years! I don't believe it!"

"You don't, hey? If you're so smart, how come you're up there and cain't get down? How come you don't grow wings?"

The boy said nothing. The old gent grinned. "I hit. Just yesterday up that canyon I hit big. I been wrong a hundred times, but not this glory hole. She'll assay out five hundred dollars a ton if she will a nickel. What I been waitin' for all my life. I laid up my markers an' put my name in a can an' I'm goin' to Prescott to get a claim down on paper. An' you're the only one knows."

"But what about me?"

The prospector raised his legs, swung round, let himself down with a grunt between Maxine and the tank, and worked himself back into his boots, bare muddy feet and all. From a pocket he took a plug of tobacco, jawed off a chunk, chewed on it awhile, thinking, then ptooed a fine stream of juice into the water.

"Well, dear boy, I rightly got to kill you."

The boy gaped. The old gent was mad as a hatter. They all were, he understood—this cuckoo, vanishing breed; they had to be to endure the life they lived. And that face turned up to him—it wasn't the face of evil either. All it evidenced was greed, friendlessness, and long years of bad luck and fried food.

"Kill me!" he cried. "What for?"

"Makes sense, don't it? Take me three days to Prescott, me an' Maxine. Meantime your daddy comes for you an' you tell him an' there she goes. He tears down my markers an' puts up his own an' he's in town by truck afore me. An' there she goes."

"I promise I won't, I promise!"

"Promises." From a ragged bedroll atop the pack the prospector took a mean-looking lever-action rifle, a .30-30 powerful enough to sink a battleship. "Partners promised me an' women promised me an' the mountains promised me an' if I had all them promises

I'd be rich but I ain't."

The boy was certain he was about to cry again. He pitied the man, but he pitied himself more. "But I don't want your claim! Neither does my father! You can't just plain murder me!"

"Why not? Here I strike it rich after tryin' till I got one foot in the grave an' here's a dear boy says no, you help me an' stay poor. Crazy man might do it, but no man in his right mind. So I let a little air in you, why not? What do I lose?"

"Why, why," the boy stammered, "why—everything!"

The old gent chuckled. "Lost that long ago." He checked the magazine of the rifle. "Dear boy, there's a sight of boys out west, but dickens little' ore any more. Survival of the fittest, an' I'm fitter'n you. Besides, if I was to count the killin's done for gold I'd also be rich but I ain't." Satisfied the weapon was loaded, he levered a cartridge into the chamber. "But I'm goin' to do it kind an' merciful. It'll hurt me longer'n it will you."

He put the rifle to his shoulder and aimed and his derby fell off.

"Dang hat." He picked it up, set it between Maxine's ears, and raised the rifle again. "Eyes ain't what they used to be neither, but what is? You set right where you be, dear boy, hold still, smile pretty, and

I'll supply you a real set of wings."

So wide and black the muzzle mouth seemed to the boy, so lunatic everything the prospector said and did, so totally improbable the situation that he might have laughed even as he flung himself backward had it not been for the report of the rifle and the split of wood beside him and the birds flying out. He flopped this way and that to make a moving target. Bullets ripped up through the planking inches from him. Lead flattened against the fan and careened off. It was like being in a battle unarmed against an entire army.

One! Two! Three! Four! Five terrible times! Then a pause. I've got to play dead, he realized, take a chance and play dead or he'll climb up and make sure. He let out a dreadful, make-believe groan and fell forward so that one hand hung limp and lifeless over the edge of the platform.

Silence.

"You dead, dear boy?"

He held his breath. He heard still another cartridge levered into the chamber. Oh, no, he yelled inside— he's going to shoot at my hand!

"Lessee now."

Whang! The bullet kissed hot the side of his thumb. No skin was broken, no blood drawn, but it took every iota of his self-control to keep from withdrawing the hand.

"Guess you be," he heard the old gent mumble. "Sorry, dear boy."

He continued to lie motionless until the prospector and his burro paraded off over the mesa toward the snake track through the Dientes.

It's a good thing I'm a goner anyway, he thought. Because if I did pull through I'd tell it and nobody would believe me and I wouldn't blame them. He shifted his head slightly to listen to the clink, clink of the frypan, receding, and to the song:

> *"Maxine, my queen,*
> *Lead me to gold,*
> *I'll deck you in dia–minds,*
> *Afore we grow old."*

A whish of air, a dark passage. Two black, ugly vultures circled near the tower, the sun shining through their wings. Vultures were a sign of something dead or something about to die. After a long look-see, first at him and then at the scatter of stones made by the coyotes, they dropped down for those leavings of rabbit the ants had not yet carried away. In this country, nothing went to waste. For him they would wait a bit.

He straightened up. Birds meant nests and nests meant eggs and eggs were food. He had food right here on this tower! He hesitated. To keep from starving, could he eat birds' eggs raw?

He turned onto his stomach and using his arms twisted to the edge of the platform above the ladder. Out flew the mother finch, but sure enough, there was her nest in the angle and in it were the two tiny eggs he'd noticed yesterday.

So near and yet so far—near enough to taste and yet too far to reach without losing balance and falling. How to do it, how? If only he could use his feet and toes to grip the pump rod, that would hold him, but the price in pain would be too great. What else, then? In his condition, the problem was as enormous as digging the Panama Canal.

Finally, amazed at his ignorance, he sat up, took off his shirt, tied one sleeve around the pump rod in the center of the platform and lay down again at the edge. Hanging onto the other sleeve like a rope, he easily stretched down to the nest, scooped up the eggs, and hauled himself upright.

Feeling as enterprising as Robinson Crusoe, he cupped the eggs and wondered if he could really get them down his gullet before they came back up. Then all at once the very hallelujah broke loose. Swooping out of nowhere, the owners fluttered round and round him, making as much ruckus as they could.

What, what, what? they seemed to tweet. Steal our

eggs? The only thing lower than a rustler or a murderer is an eggnapper! What do you want them for—Easter?

"No, to eat," he tried to reply, but his mouth and throat were so dry he could only whisper. "I'm starving."

That gave them fits. To eat? To eat? To sit right there in front of us and eat? Shame, shame! What would your mother say?

When they saw that they weren't persuading him by being furious, both small birds settled down across from him. The male was rigged out in a red cap and vest, while the female wore more modest grays and browns. Impatiently they pecked at the platform.

Can't we talk this over sensibly? asked the male. My name is Finch, and this is my wife. Meet the missus.

"Howdy, ma'am."

Maybe we're not making ourselves clear. That silly shooting a while ago has us a little upset and confused. But if you were to eat those eggs, you'd have them on your conscience as well as your stomach.

"I would?"

Of course. That's our family.

"Oh. But if I don't eat them, I may die."

Two wrongs don't make a right, the lady reminded him. As a mother, I beg you to put them back.

He looked at the eggs and then at the parents. They

looked sadly at the eggs and then at him.

"Well," he said, wavering.

Please, she said. They're getting cold.

"I did something yesterday I've been sorry about," he began.

The male shook his head. We know. That poor rabbit.

Dreadful, his wife agreed. A mere child.

"I'd like to make up for that," he whispered. "But I am so hungry. So hungry."

We'll feed you, promised the finches. Just put back our family and we'll bring you seeds and some absolutely delicious insects! We'll be your feathered friends.

He gave in. "All right, then, I will." And he did, letting himself down again by means of the shirt. The female settled herself primly into the nest and her husband flew off tweeting his thanks.

Promises, the old gent had said. His feathered friends brought him nothing.

Hope. He'd given up hope. It was working out exactly as he'd guessed. They were riding from windmill to windmill on the wrong side of the Box O. Not before night, when they returned to the ranch and parleyed with Beans, would they catch on to their mistake. Not before tomorrow morning would they ride out again, this way. That would be too late.

Voice. He could no longer even whisper. His vocal cords were dried out, his tongue was locked the way a mill locked if it wasn't greased. When you lost the power of speech, you couldn't prove you were a person.

Cattywampus. Rather than pricked with pins, his legs were being beaten with clubs. Each blow sent a bolt of agony upward through his whole body and almost knocked him cattywampus.

Sign. Now the vultures circled over him. In this country they were a sign of something dead or something about to die.

Stake. The tower was a stake and he was being burned at it the way they used to burn saints and anybody else handy.

Seeing things. Heat pouring down from the sun was reflected by the ground, and the entire mesa from mountains to mountains seemed to tip. The cattle seemed to be drifting in over an earthquake toward the tower. A horse seemed to be among them, saddled. He was seeing things.

Saliva. If he could make some saliva in his mouth he could free his tongue and speak and say who he was. By hearing who he was he'd know he still existed. But there was no moisture in him; he couldn't even sweat.

Limits. There are limits of endurance beyond which

the body cannot pass. He was fifteen years old. He was not yet fully grown or formed. He'd been more than a day and a half without food and more than a day without water. His legs were broken. He'd been left to die and left for dead. There are limits, too, beyond which the mind cannot be asked to go.

Pebble. He'd read somewhere or heard that if you were dying of thirst you could put a pebble in your mouth and the saliva would commence to flow and it was practically as satisfying as a river. He had a pebble.

From his pants pocket he took the mad stone Beans had given him. It was a little brown stone about an inch across and shaped like a heart, found only in the paunch of a white deer. When placed on a wound or a snake bite, it was supposed to draw the poison out, and it would also reduce fever. In the good old days the cowboys put great faith in it, and would ride for miles to reach one in an emergency. Now they knew doctors were trustier. Beans, though, was very superstitious. He believed in it. Making a gift of it had been parting with one of his dearest possessions.

The boy stared at it. Why was it called a mad stone? Because you were mad if you believed in it? Or because you might go mad, crazy, loco, like the prospector, if you used it?

He had to try.

Forcing the stone between his tongue and the roof

of his mouth, he sucked. It hurt. He sucked harder, like a baby on a bottle, and suddenly—blessed Mississippi! The juice of life itself ran down his throat. His tongue squirmed.

"Hu, hu," he said. "Ihu, Ihu," he said. And then, "I, I." The accomplishment thrilled him. "I! I!"

He took out the mad stone. "I can talk, I can talk!" he jabbered. "3–175, 3–175!"

The cracked, wonderful sound carried out over the mesa, to the ends of the earth it seemed. The vultures circling above him flapped away in defeat. He almost cackled with pleasure. How heavenly to hear your own voice! Except for his legs, he felt better all over. He swallowed and swallowed and spat splendidly over the edge of the platform and clutched the stone as though it were a nugget of gold. To think he'd been afraid he'd go out of his head. Why, he was as calm and collected as the day he was born.

"I would like to eat some ice cream," he announced to nobody in particular. "I scream, you scream, we all scream for ice cream."

Nor had he been seeing things. The cattle were coming in to the tank, forty or fifty of them, mostly mothers with new-branded calves, a lordly bull or two, a few heifers. They plodded in and gathered around the tower like an audience awaiting a speech.

"Ahem, ahem." He cleared his throat, stood up,

removed his stovepipe hat, adjusted his tie, and raised a hand for silence. "Ladies and gentlemen. I am Warren G. Harding, President of the United States, and I'd like to have some ice cream."

And sure enough, there was Dub in the audience. "Nice to have you with us, Dub, glad you could come. The capital of Vermont is Montpelier."

He didn't seem to be keeping their attention. They chewed their cuds and flicked their tails at flies and some had the gall to be slupping out of the tank. He'd have to do something sensational.

Extending one arm and a forefinger, he pointed at them in the orator's favorite gesture. "I claim I'm getting something that ain't due me. But I guess that every man up here says the same thing, so that don't cut no figure." He lowered his voice softly, sorrowfully. "It's all over. Tell the boys I died game and like a man."

"Mooooooo," they bawled. They were touched. They lifted their white faces and chewed sympathetically. He had them in the palm of his hand. It was the right moment to launch the burden of his address.

"Mother, why did you have to die? Kids back East read about the romance of the West but that West is gone, vamoosed, and today it's dull as dishwater. No excitement, no adventure. Get up, ride the mills, go to bed, get up, ride the mills, go to bed—nothing ever happens. Beans is more a father to me than my own father is! Now friends, about girls. If they aren't a caution. You can't live with 'em and some say you can't live without 'em. I admit I don't know. But I do know when you get to a certain age you have to make up your mind. Either they're as good-for-nothing as a calf that won't fatten or they're important. Now there's this girl in my class at school, Maxine—no, Virgie, her name is—don't you dare laugh at the President of the United States! Why do you think we're keeping you up here on this mesa? So you can live the life of Riley? Not by the hair on my chinny-chin-chin! I've pretty soon got to start shaving. We're fattening you so when you look to be a thousand pounds we can drive you to Prescott and ship you to California to a stockyard. Would you care to hear what they'll do to you there? Hamburger! Father, why can't I live in your house with you, where the books are? Why do I have to live in the bunkhouse and read catalogues? You don't have to put your arms around me and make over me. Just praise me once in a while—that isn't being sissy, to say a kind word. Father, why can't we be friends?"

The speaker grew hoarse. He stuck the mad stone back in his mouth and sucked, "Mmmmm, mmmmm, mmmmm." He mustn't lose his audience to flies. Besides, he still had to reveal his awful, unspeakable secret—the second of the three things he talked about so much to himself.

"Ladies and gentlemen," he resumed, "I'm going to let you in on a big secret. It's been under my hide for a year now, like a screw-worm gets under your hide and pesters. It's also the real reason why Beans and the hands call me 'Whichaway.' I have to tell somebody or bust. Maybe I am a rancher's son. Maybe I am supposed to grow up to be a rancher and take over the brand. But I'm also a different kind of critter, a maverick. I don't ride or rope or shoot very well and I can't help it if I'm skinny and not too strong and my eyes aren't too good and I'm clumsy. Besides, I don't care."

He lifted his head. Sunlight flashed from the rims of his specs. His voice jumped to a shout. The words spilled swiftly. "The truth is, friends, I don't want to be a rancher, even if it breaks my father's heart if he's got a heart. I've got something else in my craw and every young person ought to have the chance to decide what he's cut out for. I'm fifteen now and I have to decide whichaway I'm going to go—be what everybody expects out here or be what I really want. And friends, what I want is outlandish—you bet it is. Why, in a few years people won't even know how the Crittendens died or where they're buried. But I know —I'm carrying history around with me and I want to pass it on. Hamburger! I want to be what only women are supposed to be in the West, what my mother was. I'll say it right out loud. I want to be a school teacher —a history teacher!"

Applause deafened him, dizzied him. Cheers rocked Crazy Men Mesa. Calves were raised for him to kiss. A brass band struck up "The Stars and Stripes Forever." It was one of the finest speeches ever made by a President of the United States.

When he came to, it was nearly sundown. You fainted again, he thought, but how I wish you'd died so you wouldn't have to face another night alone up here.

At the other end of him the heavy, swollen things which had been his legs itched and throbbed. Why did you dodge those bullets? Why weren't you allowed to die quickly? You've earned it. If you were man enough you'd just push yourself off this tower. Thirty feet is far enough to drop. Boom, and it would be over. Or after dark, when the wind comes up and the mill starts to work, just sit close to the fan, count to three, and stick your head into the blades. Snick, no head.

Should I pray? Should I ask God to please put an end to me? No. That would be cowardly. It's not His fault I'm up here.

He lay on his stomach, one cheek against the hard,

weathered, bullet-torn planking, and watched the sun wink out behind the Dientes. Once again their shadows crept across the plain.

Full of delicious insects, Mr. and Mrs. Finch went to bed under him, their promise forgotten. Well, they had their own family to take care of. His cheek ached, for it seemed to him he'd been in this position all day. To relieve his cheek, he turned his head to the other side so that with one eye he could look down over the edge. There was good old faithful Dub, standing by the tank directly below him. Strange, he seemed to remember someone—the rustlers—sending him away at a gallop. Good old horse.

"Dub," he whispered, "what're you waiting for, a streetcar?"

It was then, while he looked down upon the horse with one eye, that the idea began to form, a piece here, a piece there, stuttering in his mind. If you could. Then you might. Do this next. But what about? Sure. If that worked, then you could. Or else.

He wasn't excited. He lay thinking about it as he might have a story. What was the use? He was too weak to carry it through all the way. He could do some of it, though, the first part. Then it occurred to him that even if he couldn't finish, if he at least started, when they found him tomorrow they'd know he hadn't given up. They'd say of him that he died trying to grow up and amount to something. That was how he'd be remembered.

"You can go into the ground two ways," Beans said sometimes. "You owin' the world or the world owin' you. Don't you go owin'."

The boy pushed himself into a sit, got out his jack-knife and opened it. Unbuttoning the fly of his Levis, he cut them down the crotch and slit both legs as though he were skinning himself. Next, despite the pain, he raised up enough to pull the pants from under him and bring them in a bundle into his lap.

Suddenly he realized it all depended on Dub. Popping the mad stone into his mouth he sucked until the saliva flowed. Removing it, he leaned forward. "Horse, you listen to me."

Dub's ears perked.

"Dub, I've got an idea. I know how to get myself down from this tower. Maybe. I can't do it alone and that's where you come in. So you listen, you old crow bait, you old amigo of mine. You stay right where you are tonight, right near me, savvy? Don't you go galli-vanting. And if I'm still alive when there's enough light to see by, well. . . . If I could get down on my knees and beg, I would, Dub, but I can't.

"Horse," he said with a catch in his voice, "horse, I have to have you here."

Night

Night

There was no wind this second night. The mill did not turn. A coyote howled. Others answered.

By the half-moonlight, upon his tower, the boy began to work. With his jackknife he cut the tops from his boots, cut the leather into narrow strips, and notched the strips at top and bottom. Then, except for notching, he did likewise with his pants, being careful not to waste the material. He would have to use every scrap, every thread, of everything he had. If the platform was thirty feet from the ground, and the saddle on Dub was four feet off the ground, four subtracted from thirty was twenty-six. By his reckoning the rope, or rather the line, he was making had to be twenty-six feet long.

But his arithmetic was slow and confused. He kept mixing up the numbers in feet with the numbers on the license plate, 3–175. The bolts of pain up his legs, though not as frequent now, were fiercer. They shook him. He had to grind his teeth. And while he was tying together the first part of the line, a strip of pants onto a strip of boot leather by means of the notches, he noticed that he felt light and floaty and hot and cold. He touched his forehead. Fever—he was burning up with fever. To reduce it, he put the mad stone in his mouth and went on working.

Fever made him think of the Great Prescott Fire of 1900. He hadn't been there, of course, but Beans had, and he told the story at the drop of a hat. The boy knew it word for word. How he'd like to be a teacher and tell it himself to roomfuls of youngsters who otherwise might never hear about it. What a rannicaboo!

Beans had been sitting in a quiet palace of pleasure on South Montezuma Street, which was known as "Whiskey Row," and twiddling his thumbs, he claimed. A game of poker was going on in one corner, a crap game in another, and a couple of dogs were having a free fight under a billiard table. Up went the cry, "Fire! Fire!"

It spread and rampaged all that night, July fourteenth. Four companies of volunteer firemen, the Dudes, the Toughs, the OK's and the Hook and Ladders, couldn't put it out because there wasn't enough water in the town wells to raise pressure in their hoses. To stop it, buildings had to be dynamited. By morning, two-thirds of Prescott had gone up in smoke, and the miracle was, few people gave a hoot.

Since it was Saturday night, the saloons and gambling halls had been filled with miners and cowboys who decided, as the fire spread, to make the best of a bad situation. Out of the saloons, which were going to be blown up anyway, they lugged the kegs of whiskey, out of the general stores tin cups, and out of the gambling dens the faro and roulette tables—all to the plaza, or town square. They bashed in the heads of the kegs with axes and filled their cups. Gamblers opened their tables for business as usual. And there in the center of Prescott, by the light of the flames, to the booms of dynamite blasts, they drank and gambled and joined with veteran soldiers recently home from the Spanish-American War in singing the popular song of the day, "There'll Be a Hot Time in the Old Town Tonight!"

History was what you read about, yes. But it was also what you heard about, from people who'd been there when it happened, and he, born just after the big show was over, was like a living, breathing, walking library of information. When Beans and the other old-timers were gone, couldn't he make the Old West come alive for kids, though! Couldn't he make their hair stand right on end!

All at once his own hair prickled. Why?

Now he broke out in goose bumps all over. Fever? No.

He had the strange sensation he was no longer alone.

His eyes adjusted by this time to the half-moonlight, he peered out from the tower. Dub was having a midnight snack of grass not far away. The cattle were peaceable.

He tied the last strip of leather onto a strip of pants and the rest of the pants strips together. His shirt was next. Taking it off, he cut the first long strip from the tail.

He listened. The coyote chorus had stopped. Silence surrounded him.

Suddenly a calf wailed, then another and another. Mamas started to round up their offspring. Bulls and heifers and then the whole outfit bunched, milled and stomped for a minute, then stood without moving, heads up, the calves out of harm's way in the middle of the bunch.

The boy sat rigid, scared to his very spizzerinctum. Only one thing would spook cattle like that. Only one thing would shut up a coyote. A lion. A mountain lion.

There were a lot of them on the Box O. Two or

three times a year, after the hands had chanced onto a half-eaten calf, his father would send for the hunter who lived over at Horsethief. The man would come with his horses and pack of trained hounds and guns and in a couple of days, sometimes sooner—one less lion, one more rug, and a bounty of seventy-five dollars for the hunter from the State of Arizona. A lion the hunter said, would kill fifty deer a year. When they were in short supply, he'd help himself to a calf.

The boy had seen many a nice dead kitty brought in tied over a saddle, dusty and bloody and torn by the hounds after it had been shot out of a tree, but never one alive. The back of his neck told him he was about to. Cautiously, painfully, he turned to look down and behind him.

The cat was beautiful and awful. He stood in the mouth of the same hairpin canyon out of which the prospector had appeared, watching the spooky cattle, his tail twitching. A big tom, he was probably ten feet long from nose to tail tip and weighed perhaps two hundred pounds. The boy marveled at him, unafraid now. Lions never attacked men unless cornered. Lions seldom climbed ladders.

The tom crept toward the tower, catlike and low but stalking with a limp, a hitch. The boy was sorry for him the way he'd been sorry, for a moment, for the old gent whose hitch was in his head. A bullet's smashed his shoulder, he thought, but he got away somehow and now he can't hunt deer, he's too slow, he's as crippled as I am and just as hungry. Nearer and nearer the tom came, unaware that he, too, was being watched. He crouched behind a corner of the water tank like a cat mousing.

Leaning, looking down, all at once the boy gasped.

Dub was moseying toward the tank to wet his whistle.

Lower the lion crouched.

If a lion couldn't catch a deer he'd try for a calf and if he couldn't catch a calf he'd attack a full-grown cow or a horse. One leap and he'd sink his fangs into Dub's throat and hang on till the crazed horse grew weak from loss of blood, stumbled, sank, was finished!

Dumb, unsuspecting, everybody's-my-pal Dub.

The boy snatched up his knife. But if he threw it!

Here came Dub.

He opened his mouth. But if he warned Dub away!

With all his strength the boy hurled the knife at the lion, missing by a mile, and screamed at the horse: "Dub, go home!"

Lion, horse, boy—each was as surprised as the other. The big cat leaped as though someone had stepped on his tail and with a yowl was gone. Dub reared and whinnied off into darkness on the gallop, hoofs

74

drumming.

And only then did the boy comprehend fully what he'd done. Without a knife he couldn't make a line! Without a horse he couldn't get down whether he made a line or not! But there hadn't been time to think. To save the life of an old cayuse he'd thrown and screamed away the chance, maybe, to save his own life.

"Come back, Dub," he whispered. But Dub wouldn't. He did what he was told. A pal he might be, but he wasn't smart enough, human enough, to disobey an order.

A breeze stirred. The blades of the fan began to turn, the pump rod to squeak, and water to trickle and splash from the pipe into the tank. Out on the mesa the cattle quieted down and scattered. Some coyotes resumed choir practice.

The boy sat for a long while as though made of wood, a part of the platform. Then it occurred to him that he never had expected to save himself, really, that he'd been making a line only to leave them proof he hadn't run out of sand to the very last. He took up his shirt again. Gripping the edge of the tail with his teeth, he pulled. It hurt his teeth, but the denim, softened by many washings, did rip and he could then use his hands to tear off another strip. It might be that he could do the whole shirt. His lips, cracked from dryness, began to bleed. He licked them gratefully. Nothing helps you, and nobody, he thought; you have to do everything yourself. Make your own spit, drink your own blood.

"That's what I like about Virgie. She's independent," one of him said out loud to the other. This was the third thing he talked to himself about.

"Ask if you can carry her books for her and she says thanks very much but I'll manage. And when you're talking, she looks you right in the eye. She doesn't giggle and blush the way the other girls do. If you said to her, on the way home from school, Virgie, if I had my druthers, I druther be a teacher than a rancher, she'd say well, then, why don't you? If you also said, man-to-man, Virgie, the truth is I'm getting right nigh-on to being pretty nearly practically almost just about sweet on you, she'd look you right in the eye and say partner, glad to hear it, shake. And if you turned up your toes, she'd come to your funeral, and the best thing was that she wouldn't carry a lily and turn on the waterworks and carry on like a sick chicken. She'd be sad but she wouldn't cry a drop."

Since they were seamed, the collar and cuffs of the shirt were the most difficult to tear. And since he had only teeth for a knife, the strips were irregular in width, some only a few threads wide. When his jaws began to ache from strain, he stopped and tied. On and on he worked till the shirt was done, and then he began to gnaw and rip away at his filthy socks. He didn't notice that the moon waned. He felt funny in the head again, probably from the fever.

3–175, 3–175.

He seemed to remember making a speech yesterday afternoon and talking with birds.

Or was it this afternoon? What day was it? Tuesday? How long had he been up on the tower?

My bottom is sore.

Magnetic cactus.

From sitting my bottom is sore.

Why Beans didn't join the Rough Riders.

Sore my bottom is from sitting.

"Ha–ha." It was a harsh cackle, not a real laugh.

Animals kill for food, not for gold.

Ice cream, you scream, we all scream from gangrene.

"Ha–ha–ha."

Do you scream when they cut off your legs?

There. Tie on the strips of socks. Ugh. Nothing more tasty than chewing on your own socks.

A long line but not long enough. Neckerchief next.

Whenever he thought about Beans's story about why he hadn't fought in the Spanish-American War he had to laugh. It was a ringtail snorter. It was a double-barreled whopper. Stories like it would be lost forever, language and all, if he didn't preserve them in his memory and pass them on to others.

In 18 and 98, just twenty-five years ago, Beans was a dashing young cowpuncher on the Lazy X, full of vim and vinegar. When the war with Spain broke out, Teddy Roosevelt sent a man to the Arizona Territory to enlist a squadron of men for the 1st United States Volunteer Cavalry, later known as the Rough Riders, and later than that, famous as the regiment which sailed to Cuba and charged up San Juan Hill with Colonel Teddy.

"I figgered t'sign up an' win thet war by myself," Beans would begin, "so I forks up on my hoss an' lights out like I was fightin' bees. It was twenty mile from the Lazy X t'Prescott, but I never made 'er."

"Why not?" To keep his tongue greased, you were supposed to ask the proper question at the proper moment.

"Magnetic cactus," he'd say.

"Magnetic cactus? What's that?"

"Well, you know magnetism, sort of like ee–lec–tric–ty?"

You nodded.

"An' the saguaro?"

You nodded. The saguaro was the biggest, most amazing cactus in the world, and found only in Arizona. It took them a hundred years to reach full growth, sometimes thirty feet high and four feet around and weighing more than a ton, their trunks and arms covered with sharp spikes.

"Well, b'tween the Lazy X an' Prescott there's a sight of copper under the ground an' a passel of saguaros on top. In those days, b'fore the mines dug up so much of it, the roots of them cactus growed right down t'thet copper an' drawed up the magnetism from it an' stored it up like a storage batt'ry in a truck or automobubble. Why, some of them cactus was so chock-full of magnetism they shook like a shimmy-dancer! Some of 'em was charged positive an' some was charged negative, so some pulled an' some pushed off. You come too close to a positive one an' you know what happened?"

"What?"

"Fffffffft! You'd be yanked right up to it an' stuck on them spikes. The arms'd fold aroun' you an' crush you, an' your body'n bones'd be squshed to a pulp! Then you'd be et."

"Et?" Your eyes were supposed to pop.

"Dee–voured! Why, I seen it happen t'birds, colts, calves, an' once a greenhorn friend of mine. Fffffffft! Grabbed an' stabbed an' crushed an' squshed t'juice an' et by a cactus. What a orful tradegy!" Beans would fold his arms around himself and make a crushed face and let out heart-rending groans. "An' come too close to a negative one—thoooooom! You'd be throwed off like out of a slingshot."

He'd be still a bit till you digested the horrid picture.

"Well, like I say, I was slappin' leather t'get t'Prescott an' sign up an' win the war. So I thinks, I'll jes' cut cross country an' get there quicker, so I swang off the road. In them days I wasn't allus sure whichaway I was goin' nuther.

"Anyhoo, I cuts through them magnetic cactus. Goin' like Billy–be–danged I ride right smack b'tween a positive an' a negative an' whoa! The hoss, he's big an' strong an' keeps on goin' but me, I'm stuck. The positive's pullin' and the negative's pushin' an' I'm caught in the middle an' tied like I was lassoed. An' all thet magnetism shootin' through me—whooooeee, it was a caution! I was there a hull day an' night till somebody come by an' took word t'the ranch an' you know how I was got loose?"

"Do. tell."

"They brung up a team of mules an' throwed me a rope an' drug me loose like a cork out'n a bottle. An' by the time I gets t'town, the troops was all signed up. So Uncle Sammule had t'fight the war without me—it's a wonder we come out on top. After thet, though, I could lick any man in the Terr-tory. Anyone laid a hand on me an' he was shocked flat-bang on his seater!"

"How come?"

"Kep' myself charged up with magnetism."

"How?"

"Pocketfulla copper pennies."

When the stars came out and the black of night was
washed into gray, the boy did not even know or care.
The world in which he existed was too small to have a
sky. For the fifteen-year-old who once rode the mills
there had been a nation, a state, a town, a ranch.
Then he climbed a ladder, and the world became a
high and lonely mesa four miles long and two miles
wide. This, too, had shrunk, to a platform four feet
square, a wooden raft cast away on a sea of air. Now
even that was gone. His world was as small as his own
skin and skull. Outside them, someone's teeth tore at a
red neckerchief like an animal's at food, someone's
hands twisted and ripped the cloth, someone's fingers
fashioned knots. The someone's name was "I" or
"You."

You're making a line. I've used your boots and pants
and shirt and neckerchief and the line isn't long
enough to reach the saddle on my horse.

You've got my underwear, your B.V.D.'s. Using them
might.

But then I'd be down to the bare facts.

But I'll be dead so why do you care if I'm found

naked?

Why don't you use the top half of my B.V.D.'s and leave the rest on? I couldn't get your B.V.D. legs off over my legs anyway.

Take your hands and tear the B.V.D.'s around my waist and back and pull the top off over your shoulders. There.

But if my idea should work you'll be upright after a while and the bottom of my underwear will fall off.

Be modest. Be a modest corpse. At least tighten up the cloth around my waist and tie a knot in it to keep yourself covered. All right.

Now tear the top of my B.V.D.'s into very thin strips. All right.

Now tie them together. All right.

There. See what a nice long line I've made. Do you think it's long enough?

Only one way to find out. Try it.

Who, me?

No, you.

Oh.

Day

Day

But when he lay flat and turned over on his stomach and put his head over the rim of the platform, he ducked it back at once, astonished. Someone was looking up at him.

He risked another peek. It was a boy, a boy's face on the water of the tank. And the boy on the water forced the boy on the tower out of his skin and skull, out of his self, out of the cave in which he'd hidden like a wounded animal, and drove him out into the world of time and place and other existences once more.

Why, it was the middle of the morning. The sun was high and hot. This was the second morning. He'd been up here almost two days and all of two nights.

And down below, grazing near by, was a horse, his horse. He'd been smart enough not to go home when he was told.

And what was in the water was a reflection. Dirty and bespectacled and sunburned and wild it might be, but the face was his.

"Howdy," he said out loud. "I know you. Howdy."

Only his face was reflected, but he could imagine what the rest of him resembled. A half-naked, half-dead scarecrow, a rag, a bone, a hank of hair. Below the knees he was afraid to imagine. "Dub," he said, "Dub, my turtledove, come here."

The horse flicked his ears and started.

"Ho. Right there. That's it. Right under me. I'm going to try that idea. They won't get here before noon and when they do I won't know it, but we'll show them something. So don't you move, don't even bat an eye. This time I mean it."

Dub in place, he reached behind him for the line. Surely it was the strangest lifeline anyone had ever put together—boot strips tied to shirt strips tied to pants strips tied to sock strips tied to neckerchief strips tied to B.V.D. strips tied, at the very end, to the wire handle of the grease bucket which he'd bent into a hook. Lying flat, he let it down hand-over-hand, slowly, carefully, for everything went with it. If it should snag on the timbers of the tower, he was lost. Down it went, directly over the horse. He came to the boot strips and pants strips, to the end. He lowered his arm and hand. He stretched. Then he burst into a sob.

The wire hook dangled six inches above Dub's saddle.

Six inches from maybe. It was too much to bear, especially when he'd already borne more than a boy should be required to. A whole night's toil, cutting and ripping till his gums were sore and his lips had cracked and bled, only to have it wasted.

He lay sobbing. The sun seared his bare skin. Tears ran down his cheeks. Transferring the wetness to his lips with his fingers he smudged the lenses of his specs.

His specs!

He sat up, drew up the line, coiled it in his lap, and took off his glasses and examined them. Suppose, besides the bucket handle, he used his specs? Suppose he bent one steel bow straight and let the curve of the other bow serve as a hook? Wouldn't that add six inches to his line?

He had to try. First he untied the wire handle hook, straightened it in the center and made right angles at each end, then tied it into the line farther up. Next, he bent one bow of his specs forward, taking great pains not to snap it off at the hinge. He tied it onto the last B.V.D. strip at the end of the line. The other bow, at its normal backward angle below the rim, formed a kind of hook. A kind of. Lying flat, he let the line down again. Now it had to be long enough, it had to.

There. The line hung straight. And it would reach, it would. With his hand he moved the line closer to the saddle. It was like fishing, only with the bow of a pair of specs for a fishhook, and what he was fishing for was the coil of rope on Dub's saddle.

Every working saddle was equipped with a coil of rope, but his was rigged with two coils tied together, a mass of hemp too thick to unstrap easily. He carried the double coil for protection. If you didn't rope well, and the hands were always daring you to show what you could do, you could just point to the double coil as though it was too much bother to unstrap. Such a trick had spared him a lot of embarrassment. Now it might spare him more than that.

But first he had to fish for and catch the rope strap in order to free the double coil. This leather strap was attached at one end to the saddle by a D-ring, was wound around the coil, and its other end was looped over the saddle horn. He must hook the loop and lift it over the horn. If he figured right, the weight of the double coil would then unwind the rope strap and allow the rope to fall from the saddle to the ground, where he could get at it.

He jiggled the line. He squinted down. He groaned. He couldn't see! There were his specs at the end of the line and without them he could scarcely see a fly on the end of his nose. Talk about dumb boys and smart horses!

Well, he'd do it by feel. With his hand he jiggled and twitched and fiddled the line over the saddle horn. It went taut. That might be the loop. Now to lift without breaking the line. He held his breath and raised it an inch, two, three. Release! The line swung. And he couldn't even see.

Quickly he hauled it up, untied his specs from the end and bent the bow back in place. It wasn't quite even with the other one, and when he put the glasses on they were crooked, but now he could see, could look down and see to his joy that the weight of the double coil had indeed unwound the rope strap, and there on the ground was the rope and there at one side was the knotted end.

He'd done it! Pretty slick for a book boy. Now all he had to do was make a slipknot in the end of his line, drop it down over the knot end of the rope, hitch it up tight, and raise the rope loop by loop to the platform.

"No!" he gasped. "Oh, you dumb whichaway!"

Because the double coil was on the ground now, four feet below the saddle. His line was only twenty-six feet long and to reach the rope it would have to be thirty feet and he'd used every smithereen of everything he had.

But wait. Wasn't there? Hadn't he seen? He dragged himself to the other side of the platform and hung his head over. Sure enough, there was Mrs. Finch sitting on her eggs and among the twigs and grass of the nest were some pieces of string.

But now he had no shirt sleeve to tie around the pump rod. Well, he'd have to rely again on his own line. He sat up and untied a knot to separate its strongest part, the strips of leather and pants. One end of this shorter length he tied around the pump rod and, using the same method by which he'd stolen the eggs, got a firm grip on its free end and let himself over the edge of the platform, his fingers feeling for the string in the nest.

With an angry tweet, the lady flew out, to be joined by her husband. They fluttered and scolded above him, which was no help. Down he hung, thirty feet in the air, suspended by the fragile strand. If even one strip tore, if even one knot gave way!

All at once, sweat gushed out all over him, surprising him, for it was a miracle there should be any moisture remaining in his body. Panting, sweating, he grasped the end of a piece of string, eased it out of the nest, balled it in his fingers, found another, eased that out, and a third, then hoisted himself up.

He was exhausted. If he'd been willing to bring up the whole nest, it would have been easy. He'd left it intact, however, and he hoped his feathered friends were grateful. But Mr. Finch went dipping away and his wife, with a sniff, returned to her eggs.

Untying the strong part of the line from around the pump rod, he joined it again to the rest. Then he tied the three pieces of string together—by his guess they added at least four feet—attached the additional string to the bottom of the line, and made a slipknot at the very end. He hitched himself back to the other side of the platform, and for the third time let down the line.

This would be the hardest thing of all. The double coil of rope lay on the ground beside the horse, the knot end, luckily, drooping over one side of the top coil. He must get a slipknot of string down over the knot of rope. It was like threading a needle from a distance of thirty feet. He aimed down the line. His eyes bulged.

Just as he had the slipknot dead center over the rope knot, a puff of wind blew the line to one side. The pump rod squeaked laughter. He almost cried again with vexation. He seemed to be losing control of himself.

The puff of wind steadied into a breeze. Now he

had to slant the line against the breeze by moving his arms, and when he did that he couldn't aim it down.

Five, six, seven, eight times. And there. Pull. He had it. He saw the slipknot draw tighter and tighter. The line went taut in his hands. Yes, he had it!

Now the last step. Up, up, up with the line. The rope began to rise toward him. Knot by knot, up, up. His breath whistled out of his lungs. The more rope in the air, the heavier load on the line, the greater chance of its breaking. Some of the links were little more than threads.

But he passed the boots and the pants and the shirt, and the rope continued to rise. He reached the strips of socks and B.V.D.'s and now, now—rope! He hauled away—rope, real rope!

He unwound into the second coil and through it and sitting up pulled faster and faster till there was no more rope on the ground, till he had a splendid pile on the platform, till he had to stop because he had the world in his hands.

Yes, yes, he was attached to one end of a real rope and the rope was attached to a saddle horn and the saddle was attached to Dub and good old faithful, ugly, smart, beautiful, dumb Dub was attached to the world!

The boy lay limp for a time, resting, one arm curved

around the lovely pile of rope.

So far, so good. His original idea had been to tie the rope securely to the pump rod and then, Dub standing firm, to hang from it and descend hand over hand. But he could never manage that now, he was too weak.

He thought about the rope. There must be eighty or ninety feet of it, long enough to do anything. Then he thought about the tower. And then about Dub and what he was capable of. Suddenly he pictured himself on one end of the rope, Dub on the other, and the tower in the middle.

He sat up. A pulley! He could use the whole tower as a pulley!

Feverishly he found the end of his makeshift string and cloth and leather line, untied it from the rope, and tossed it over the edge. He tied the end of the rope around his body, high up under his arms. Then he had a talk with his helper.

"Dub," he said, "now listen. You're down there and I'm up here and we're going to get together." Dub stamped a forefoot. "You do just what I say, savvy? When I say back, you back. When I say ho, you ho. When I cluck, you come ahead, but slow. Do you understand, horse?" Dub shook his head. "All right, then. Get ready. Now, back. Back, Dub."

The horse backed away from the tower, the rope

moved, the boy paid it out.

"Ho! Ho, Dub." The horse stopped. There were only a few feet of slack. Leaning, he placed the rope in the nick between two planks on the edge of the platform toward Dub, and dragged himself to the opposite side till he'd taken up the slack. Then he clucked. The horse started forward. "Two steps, Dub. Ho! Ho!"

Now, to get those big hunks of rotten meat and the rest of him over the edge and lower himself by the hands and arms and shoulders till the rope held him.

He grunted and groaned and felt himself going free. Now he was propped up on the platform only by his elbows. One hand down, now the other. Now to let go. He didn't dare look down. Nothing there but air. How would Dub behave when he felt the pull on his saddle? It had been a long time since he'd braced himself against the weight of a calf or steer.

The boy hung by his fingers. They slipped. And just as they slipped a new fear made him stiffen and claw.

Why hadn't he tested the saddle? Why hadn't he pulled against the horn before he got himself off the platform? That saddle had been on Dub for three days—what if the cinch under the animal's belly had loosened, and when he let go the whole saddle let go? Too late, too late.

He let go.

He dropped inches. The rope cut into the underflesh of his shoulders. But cinch and saddle held. Then he dangled as he had from the vane two days before, twisting and turning like an outlaw hanging from a noose. He could see beneath the platform now, could follow the rope as it ran out and down in a straight, taut line to Dub on the other side of the tower, and alongside Dub's neck to the saddle horn. The horse seemed so far away that he'd have to shout.

"C'mon now, Dub!" He clucked. "Easy, easy!"

Dub moved forward, plodding step by step, an old cow pony asked once more to play tug-of-war with a stubborn critter. The rope buzzed over the edges of the platform.

"That's it, Dub! Take your time."

Down, down, down from that terrible tower, foot by foot he descended. This was what a ride in an elevator must be like. He'd never ridden in one, for there weren't any in Prescott or for that matter in Arizona, but he'd heard that all kinds of buildings back East had them and anyone could ride them, and for free. He looked below. The ground was only feet away. In seconds he'd be standing on terra firma.

Standing! He couldn't stand. Even the thought of touching the ground with those broken, swollen legs was agony.

"Ho! Ho, Dub!" he cried.

Dub stopped, and now he dangled like a puppet on a string. But it was lucky he had stopped, for he'd been about to bump into the cross-braces between the two main upright timbers of the tower.

He twisted and turned. So near again, and yet so far. How could he possibly get down without putting his weight on his legs? Wasn't there some way he could use his arms and shoulders instead?

Suppose. What if? He'd have to, much more of this and the rope would pull his arms right out of their sockets.

Gripping the rope, he began to swing himself to and fro in a wider and wider arc, the living pendulum of a clock. When he judged the arc was wide enough, he let go of the rope, flung both arms out and wrapped them around the massive six-by-six corner timber of the tower, clinging to it as though to a tree. Now to get slack line.

"C'mon, Dub, c'mon!"

As Dub came forward, the line slithered over the platform, dropped below the boy. He slipped one arm down the weathered timber, hung on, slid the other down, hung on, repeated this over and over, gasping with the effort, sweating again, gushing sweat. And then, lifting his heavy limbs upward in a curve so that he would fall upon his back, not upon his legs, he pushed himself free.

He landed with a thud. His specs flew. For a moment he couldn't breathe, the wind was jolted out of him.

But when he knew where he was he rolled over and with a small glad whimper buried his face in dirt, and hugged the glorious round world off which he'd fallen for two awful days and nights. Making mud with his sweat, smearing his body with it, he kissed the beloved mother earth from which he had so long been separated.

He searched for his crooked specs. They were right beside him. He hooked them over his big ears even though there was nothing he wanted to see.

But he did want to say good-by to Dub while he could. He called him, and heard the clop of his hoofs coming around the tower. Trailing the rope from his horn, Dub stopped over him, so near he could reach out with one hand and pat a fetlock.

"Good old boy," he said, still lying flat on his stomach. "Good old friend. We did it. Dub, I thank you very much."

He closed his eyes. He heard the scrape of pebble against shoe as Dub lifted and put down a hoof. He listened to the purl of water from the pipe into the tank only a few cruel feet away—that water which might prolong his life for hours could he but use his legs to stand and bend over the tank.

"Dying, Dub," he mumbled into the dirt. "Too bad. All this trouble getting down."

Then he felt it. A pulse, a trembling of the ground. The surface of the mesa was like a drum. On it beat something light, something far away.

He gripped the rope trailing from Dub and hauled himself to a sitting position. He craned and peered through the cross-braces of the tower.

Riders! Three riders headed this way.

Tears filled his eyes. He wasn't going to die! They might have to cut off his legs but he'd live, he'd live to be a man and listen to Beans's whoppers and take care of Dub and tell Virgie he really was no-fooling sweet on her and someday be a teacher because his father might be one of the riders and when he saw how his son had got himself down from a windmill tower with two broken legs he'd be proud of him, he'd let him be anything he wanted.

Now the riders were less than half a mile away, beelining toward him, and suddenly he was ashamed. Nobody was going to catch him playing in the dirt like a baby. Nosiree, while he could still wiggle they were going to find him chin up and feisty and where he belonged.

Ordering Dub to ho, to stand fast, he gripped the rope hanging from the saddle horn with both hands and hauled, fell back, hauled again. This time he wrenched himself high enough to get one hand on the horn, then both. By this means, without using his legs or feet, he dragged himself to the saddle, sagging over it face down like a sack of flour. So desperate was his resolve, so near were the hoofbeats, that somehow he twisted himself about and letting both legs drop, straddled the horse. Pushing on the horn, he sat up.

Everything went black. He swayed. He thought he was fainting. But when the riders rounded the tower and reined in, his father and two of the hands, he was forked up and sitting easy.

They stared as though at a freak in a circus. Instead of the fattest man or the bearded lady, he was the world's skinniest, dirtiest, bloodiest, craziest-legged boy.

"Well?" his father said.

"Rustlers," he said. "Night before last. Two of them in a Reo truck and they killed and butchered two of our yearlings. But I got their license number. 3–175." He thought of mentioning the old gent and his claim, but decided against it. Whatever he's found, he thought, real gold or fool's gold, let him keep it. We all have to have something.

"All right," his father said impatiently. "What happened here?"

"I was greasing the mill and a dust devil hit me,

that's all. I couldn't get down till just this morning. My legs are broken."

They glanced at his legs. One of the hands whistled. The other made a face. His father glanced, then looked around at the line of shirt and pants and socks and boots and neckerchief and B.V.D.'s and string and the long rope trailing from the horn to the far side of the tower.

"You mean," he said, "it took you two whole days and nights just to figure how to get down off a mill?"

When the boy said nothing, his father shook his head. "Well, coil up. No sense leaving good rope."

The boy commenced to coil. "Could I please have some water?"

One of the hands dismounted, went to the tank, noticed the hat floating, filled it and brought it over. The boy gulped and spilled, gulped and spilled. "Look at him suck." The hand grinned. "Like a bitty calf on a milk bucket." The boy put the wet hat on his head and went on coiling.

"Killed two head, you say?" his father said. "Well, we'll get you back to the bunkhouse and call the sheriff. And the doc. Can you ride?"

"I think so."

"Then let's ride."

Dub couldn't handle the pace the three men set.

He lagged behind.

Too swollen to squeeze into the stirrups, the boy's feet banged against them. With every thump he had to hold tighter to the horn and bite his tongue to keep from crying out. He might not make the fifteen miles to the ranch, but even if he fell off he wouldn't holler. Not even for his father. Ever again. He was man enough now to cut his own mustard.

Halfway to the pass through the Butter Mountains he let his gaze sweep along them and along the Dientes and then back over a shoulder across Crazy Men Mesa to the tower. Cattle grazed. Dust devils walked. The wind blew. The mill turned.

GLENDON and KATHRYN SWARTHOUT have collaborated on one other book for young readers, *The Witch and the Magic Saber*. Glendon Swarthout has also written several novels for adults. The husband-and-wife team live in Scottsdale, Arizona.

He's just made the find of his life!

The Machine Gunners

by Robert Westall

Chas McGill already has the second-best collection of scavenged World War II souvenirs in town. But when he finds a machine gun—still attached to a Nazi fighter plane—he knows he's finally moved into first place. The bad thing is, he can't brag about it. With the help of two of his most trusted friends, Chas removes the gun and cleverly hides it from the authorities by building a secret bunker around it. But as the search for the missing gun mounts, Chas and his friends have other things on their minds. There are rumors of an imminent German invasion—and guess who plans to be ready for the counterattack?

"The best book so far written for children about the Second World War."

—*The Times* (London)

"A bloody good story!" —*School Library Journal*

Winner of the Carnegie Medal
A *Boston Globe-Horn Book* Honor Book
A Child Study Association of America
Children's Book of the Year

A BORZOI SPRINTER PUBLISHED BY ALFRED A. KNOPF, INC.